Call it Courage

Eman Ghoneim

Lexington Universal Academy

Spring 2012

Dedication

I dedicate this novel to my family, who was there for me all those nights I had trouble writing'; for my friends, who helped inspire me with some of the names for this story, and finally, for my teacher, Dr. S.

Without Dr. Simandle, I would have never written this novel, or my other two previous novels. Thank you.

Prologue

I hold my son in my arm, hoping he doesn't make a sound. I can hear the Destruction coming closer, and closer.

"Mommy, why do we have to do this all the time?" Danny whispered in a terrified voice.

"Shh, it's all right, it's almost over," I told him.

Suddenly the lights turned on.

"What happened?" my husband asked. The lights don't usually turn on until the Destruction is over, and it wasn't over yet; you could still hear the---wait. It stopped. Something is wrong.

"I'll go check it out. This is not right," Jason said.

"I'm coming too," I said.

"No, it's too dangerous,"

"I want to go,"

"Please stay here," Jason said, and he ran upstairs. I followed cautiously behind, my son still holding my hand.

When we got to the second level of the house, Jason ran straight to the window. The sky was clear, the sun was shining, and everything looked perfect. But everyone should have known better. In fact some confused people came out of their homes and into the streets.

Jason opened the door.

"You're not going out there!" I told him.

"I have to; I want to see what's going on,"

"What if it's a trap?"

Jason looked at me. "It's a risk we have to take," He hugged me tight and kissed our son Danny, on the cheek, and left the house.

You don't have to take it, I thought to myself.

"Mommy, what's going on? Why is Daddy outside?" Danny begged me.

"Don't worry; everything is going to be all right," I reassured him, but really was telling it to myself. I kept my eyes on Jason.

Suddenly, we heard a very loud

BEEEEEEEEEEEEEEEEEEEEEEEEEEEEEEE EEEEEEEEEEEEEEEEEEEEP!

Oh no! That sound only comes when an Arrest was going to happen!

"Jason!" I screamed.

I saw him look at me, say something, probably the last thing he ever said, then, BOOM!

Chapter 1

BEEEEEEEEEEEEEEEEEEEEEEEEEEEEEEP

"Ugh, not again! God this is beginning to be annoying!" I said. I ignored the sound and continued working.

"Danny, hurry! Get down here!" my mom yelled.

"What's the point of going down there? They can't take me, I didn't do anything. I'm staying here!" But I knew that's wasn't true. *They took Dad for no reason,* a voice in my head said.

"Please Danny; just come down here. Why do we have to do this every time?" Mom yelled again.

I went downstairs, not because I was scared of them, but because I knew my mom was. That was the only reason that I tried to stay out of trouble with them. I didn't want her to lose me, like she lost my dad.

***

As usual, I woke up at the same time every day for school. I did my usual routine and stepped outside and found the DOs patrolling the neighborhood, like normal. Everyone calls them the "DOs" because they are Destruction Officers, and you basically have to DO everything they say. I scowled at them behind their backs.

I met up with Nate on the way to school. Nate is my best friend, and he's also the biggest computer geek ever. But he's also pretty cool.

We got to our first class of the day without any DOs stopping us or anything. We basically just tried to avoid them as much as we could while they patrolled the hallways.

School was pretty boring, but it was boring everyday so I didn't really care. Things only got really interesting when one of the brave kids stood up to the DOs. Now, those were the best days.

I walked up to the house again, but from far away, I could tell something was going on. There were DOs everywhere in their DOCs, Destruction Officer Cars, and on foot. They seemed to be searching the house.

I broke out into a run. "Mom! Mom!" I yelled as I ran to the house. I moved past the DOs and into the house. DOs were everywhere inside. I looked frantically for my mom. Suddenly I heard her voice.

"You have no right or proof!" she yelled. The DO with her said something I couldn't hear.

I burst in the room, and as soon as I did two DOs grabbed me and pinned me to the wall. "Mom! What's going on? What happened?"

She looked at me then back at the DO. She had a sad expression on her face. "I'll come peacefully,"

The DOs holding me released me and I ran to my mom. "Where are you going? Are you being Arrested? Why?" I didn't understand anything. She was going to "come peacefully"? For what?

"Could I just say goodbye to my son?" my mom asked. The DO held up one finger signaling only one minute.

Before I could say anything, my mom whispered, "Danny, listen to me. I don't have much time to explain, remember Plan Ran?" Mom quickly looked around to see if any DOs could hear her. "I need you to do that now. Everything will be alright. And tell Nate's dad I said 836. He'll understand and he'll tell you,"

As soon as she finished the DOs came bursting in. Time was up.

"Remember Danny, whatever happens, I'll always love you," Mom said,

"I love you too, Mom," I said as they were dragging her out the door.

My first thought was, Plan RAN! Plan RAN was something my mother and I had practiced doing ever since my father was taken. If something happened, I was to Run Away to Nate's house. RAN. But I didn't know what 836 was.

I grabbed my backpack and RAN to Nate's house.

Chapter 2

By the time I got to Nate's house, I was out of breath. I could feel tears streaming down my face. I was so confused. What did Mom do? And what was 836?

I rang the doorbell. I kept on ringing until Nate's mom came and opened the door.

"Danny, what happened? Why are you crying?" she asked, he face showing her concern.

"R.A.N…836…it's Mom! They took her; they just took her! She said to tell you 863," I was really crying now. I could barely get the words out of my mouth. Nate's mom took me inside.

All of a sudden, Nate came running downstairs, followed by his dad.

"Hey Danny….whoa, what happened?" Nate asked.

"Come on we have to leave…NOW," Nate's mom said.

Nate's fathers' eyes grew wide. "Ok, let's go. Bess, get the pack. Nate, Danny, come with me," he said. He opened the door to the house and went outside to their car. Nate and I followed him.

As we sat down, Bess came running from in the house, carrying a backpack on her shoulder. Mr. Smith started up the car and started driving.

"Where are we going?" I asked mystified.

Nate looked at me. "I've done this in a drill before. I think we're going to my grandparents' house," he whispered. "It's best not to talk just in case we might be going somewhere private,"

After about 5 hours, we arrived at a garage. "This *is* my grandparents' house,"

Nate said. The garage door opened and the garage was empty. Nate's dad parked the car inside.

"Everybody get out," he said. As soon as I stepped out and they closed the garage door, Mr. Smith started walking away. We followed him. Nobody was talking, so that made me think that something BIG was happening.

We walked until we got to a dark brick house. Mr. Smith knocked on the door. I wasn't really paying close attention, but I was sure it was a special knock. A middle aged man opened the door.

"Yes?" he asked.

"It's time," Mr. Smith said.

The man did a double take, and then let us inside. Maybe he was just looking for the usual DOs?

He led the way to a room. In the room, there was an ordinarily looking office. The man reached out under the carpet and lifted a trapdoor. *What's going on?* I wondered. *Why is everyone acting all secretive? And what's with the* trap *door? I what's so secret.*

When he opened the door, there was a staircase leading down. Mr. Smith went down first. Then, Mrs. Smith, Nate, then me. The man shut the door behind me.

The staircase was cold and dark. I kept stepping down until I saw a light and Nate at the bottom.

Where are we? I mimed Nate.

He shrugged his shoulders.

When I turned toward the room, I saw other people there. There were monitors everywhere, all hooked up to other things. Screens, computers, and other devices I've never seen before.

Mr. Smith turned to us. "Welcome to Samsa,"

Chapter 3

Samsa? I thought that was a rumor. Nobody knew if Samsa really existed. They were supposedly this rebel group fighting against the Destruction. People said it was just a legend; and now they're telling me it really exists? And it's been here the whole time? Was my mom part of it?

"What are we doing here?" Nate asked.

A man appeared at the door and looked at me. "Did she tell you anything before she left?"

I turned toward him. "836,"

He looked at Mr. Smith. "We don't have enough time. We need to work right away," His tone was urgent, as if those numbers meant the worst things ever.

"Wait, what do those numbers mean?" I asked. Nobody replied to me. "What does it mean?!"

Mrs. Smith came up to me. "Come on dear, you need to rest. You've had a long day. Things will make more sense in the morning. You too, Nate,"

She led us into a different room. The basement was surprisingly big. The room had some sleeping bags and pillows all over the floor. I jumped to the nearest sleeping bag. Nate lay down beside me.

"Danny, to tell you the truth, I've known about this,"

I looked up at him. "Why did you never tell me?"

"I wasn't allowed. I haven't even been here before,"

"I still don't think that's an excuse not to tell me," I said angrily.

"Danny..."

"Good night," *Mom, where are you?*

I thought to myself as I drifted off to sleep.

Chapter 4

"Good morning," Mrs. Smith said, waking me up.

I got up and saw that everyone was sitting around a table eating breakfast. I sat down across from Nate.

"Ok, I want to know what's going on," I said firmly. The man I had seen earlier, "Hawk", spoke.

"Your mom was part of Samsa. There was something she was supposed to do, but it went wrong. She got caught by the DO and that's why they took her away. The numbers she told you is a code. Eight days, and three minutes after six o' clock,"

"And what is supposed to happen in 8 days and 3 minutes after 6 o' clock?" I asked.

"That's where we come in. We have to send someone up there to finish the job," he said.

"I suppose you knew about this too?" I ask Nate. He looked down at his plate. I rolled my eyes. "How come no one told me about this?"

"It was too dangerous; this is not the only place for Samsa's headquarters. There are places all over the nation," Hawk said.

"But your mother was going to tell you as soon as she was done with her mission," Mrs. Smith reassured me.

"The truth of it is," Nate began and I snorted at the word *truth,* "The only reason I was allowed to join was because I was able to hack into different security systems. You know my thing for computers,"

"And a very good thing it is. We wouldn't have been able to connect to the 2nd level of the Destruction system defenses without him," Hawk said. Nate beamed.

Even though I was annoyed at Nate, I couldn't help but be proud of him. He was always interested in codes and hacking into different systems.

"So do you have to do something special to join?" I asked. I was ready to fight; to get my mom and dad back.

"Are you sure you want to join? It's very dangerous and you can't just walk out of it," Mrs. Smith said worriedly.

"It's his choice," Hawk said. "If he really wants to risk it, he can; his mother knew he would be a great fighter for the team,"

His mother knew he would be a great fighter for the team.

"Then I want to join," I said firmly.

"Do you think you have what it takes to become a Samsa member?" he asked, looking at me in the eye.

"Yes,"

"Do you really want to overthrow the Destruction and help rescue your parents and everyone else that was Arrested?"

I swallowed. Then I said grimly, "Yes,"

"Then you're in,"

I'm in. I'm part of the nation-wide legendary rebel group called Samsa, whose plan is to overthrow the Destruction.

I'm in.

Chapter 5

Something beeped. Hawk pulled out his phone and turned it on. "Robin to Nest, come in Nest," the voice said. Did all of these people have bird names?

"Nest is here, this is Hawk speaking," Hawk said.

"Project X is on its way. Meet on the highest branch of the Home tree. Vultures have been scouted near the Plant. Seven three six," Robin said, and then hung up.

"Ok, what was that?" I asked.

"That was Robin," Hawk said.

"Obviously, but what's Project X, and the Plant? Who are vultures, and what is the Home tree?" I was getting really confused. Those numbers I recognized as 7 days and 3 minutes after 6 o clock.

"Robin is another one of our hackers. He programmed our phones so that whenever we call one another, the DOs can't track us or hear our conversations. It's as if we're not even using the phone," Hawk began. "We are the Nest. This place, or basically where the main movement is;

and this house is the Plant. Vultures are our name for DOs and the Home tree is the main headquarters where we plan and do everything. You'll find out what Project X is later"

"Now we need to move, immediately. We've scouted suspicious DOs near us," Mr. Smith said. Everybody got up and put the dishes away.

"My car is out back, let's go;" Hawk said.

Pretty soon we were in Hawk's car and driving away. When we finally stopped, we were at a huge building. It looked like an enormous business headquarters. Then I read the name.

Darnis? Wait isn't that—

"Mr. Smith, isn't Darnis the company you and Mom worked for?"

"Yes Danny. Not only that, but Darnis is the Home Tree of Samsa," he said.

Chapter 6

"Darnis, a business, is the headquarters of Samsa? Isn't that a little too...exposed?" I asked dumbfounded. Darnis is a really big company. It sounded a bit odd for this to be the Home Tree, since there were DOs everywhere, and they basically ran everything.

"Not at all. This way, the DOs won't suspect anything," Hawk said as a matter of fact.

"So the highest branch, is the top floor?" I guessed. I'm starting to get the hang of this code stuff.

"Exactly," Mr. Smith said, or should I say "Raven". Nate's name, I found out was Eagle. Mine is Falcon. I like that name; it makes me feel important to have my own code name.

"And up to the top floor we go," Hawk said.

****

We went up an elevator to the top floor and arrived at a big room.

"Ok here's the plan; we are supposed to have a meeting anyway, but people will be suspicious if we bring two kids along," Hawk started.

"I'm not a kid—"I tried to tell him.

"So we need Eagle and Falcon to sneak into the kitchen, and disguise themselves as waiters. That way you have a reason to come into the meeting room. Serve drinks, or refreshments, you know?" Hawk finished.

"Hawk, don't you think this is a little too dangerous for them?" Raven asked.

"No, they knew the risks they were taking when they joined. Consider this as their first mission assignment," Hawk replied, walking us to the elevator.

"We can do it," Nate said. There was a button on the elevator named kitchen.

"All right, the kitchen is two floors down from here. We'll see you guys soon," Hawk said, "And here are your new phones,"

He gave us the newest high tech phones that were almost impossible to find. Two days ago I would have jumped up and down and hugged Hawk. But things were different now. I have to find my mom, and then maybe I'll jump up and down and smile again.

"And remember, you are just starting out, so there's no need to take many risks," Raven warned as the elevator door closed.

There was something about taking risks that I just wasn't sure about...

Chapter 7

When the elevator door opened, we quickly stepped out, I'll admit, I was pretty worried. I mean, sneaking into the kitchen of a DO run building, disguising myself as a waiter, then trying to get in to a super secret meeting, held by a legendary group called Samsa, who I didn't really know existed until yesterday.

It didn't take long to find the kitchen; there was a huge sign saying KITCHEN with an arrow on it pointing the way we were supposed to go.

It was a huge kitchen. There were people everywhere, rushing about, carrying trays or putting servings on tray. I looked to my left and saw a room marked STORAGE. I grabbed Nate and we ran inside.

We were in luck or something, because the whole room was full of chef's hats and waiters' clothes. Nate and I grabbed the nearest ones that fit and went out the door,

I saw what looked like a line of waiters who seemed to be getting their orders. Fortunately, the line was short, so after the last person was in line, Nate said,

"We were supposed to deliver refreshments for the Darnis meeting on the top floor,"

The Chef's face became grim. "Who told you about that? You weren't supposed to know about that meeting!"

Luckily, I thought fast. "That's why they sent us; we're the only ones that know. *You* better not say anything about it. How did *you* know?"

The Chef's face flushed. "*I* am the Chef! I know about these things!"

He gave us platters of food and trays and we walked away.

"Step one of our mission complete. Now comes the hard part," Nate said.

We went back into the elevator and pressed the number to the highest level. When the doors opened, we walked outside until we found the room we were supposed to go to.

When we got there, there was problem. The doors were locked, and we realized there was a security scanner check and we did not have security cards.

"They could have at least mentioned this," I mumbled. "Now what?"

Chapter 8

Suddenly the door opened. A big burly man wearing a security officer's uniform opened the door. Surprisingly, he wasn't wearing the usual DO getup so I figured he wasn't a DO.

"You're late! The members are getting hungry!" he said. We were too shocked to move. "Well, come on then, don't just stand there staring. Birds don't wait in their nest for a worm to come to them."

Wait. Did he just give us a hint, or was that just a random proverb...?

I glanced at Nate but he was just as surprised. We followed the man inside. The room was really big. There was a huge table with lots of people sitting around it. Some I recognized like Hawk and Raven. As soon as he saw us, Raven breathed a sigh of relief, but Hawk showed no emotion at all. I took that as a sign that he was proud we made it.

Nate started to go run for Raven and Hawk, but I signaled to him. I pointed at the trays.

Oh, right, he lipped. We began serving all the members in the room. More people began filing in, then the meeting started.

Hawk cleared his throat. "As you all know, Mother Dove has been captured by Destruction. She gave us a number, 836, telling us the time we had. Now it is 636, telling us we only have 6 more days and a couple of hours to send someone up there. The volunteer we need has to be good hacking into different systems and software defenses. This person will also have to have a special eye implant made especially from Samsa's top surgeons and engineers. This eye implant will be our source of communication with the volunteer. The eye has a series of features including, x-ray, decoder, communicator and more. I would volunteer myself, but with the Mother gone, I need to keep things in order down here. If anyone here wants to volunteer, say so now,"

"I want to do it! I can so beat all their defenses and everything!" the voice was very close, and I turned to find Nate, his hand waving in the air.

Wait, Nate?

Chapter 9

"Absolutely not," Raven declared.

"No, I'll go; it's my mom after all," I said.

"Dan, you don't know a thing about computers," Nate said causally. He had a point. I wasn't into hacking; I just wanted my mom back.

Many other people volunteered, including Robin; or someone I was pretty sure was Robin.

"I need someone who is a hacker; I think that Eagle and Robin are our only choices," Hawk said.

"But he's just a kid!" someone shouted.

"But he knows what he signed up for, and he can do some of the best computer work I've seen," Hawk said.

"I can do it. I can hack into different systems and codes, Robin specializes in safety security," Nate said.

"I guess he's right; that's more my thing," Robin stated.

"So it's agreed. Eagle will infiltrate the Destruction from the inside, while we plan our attack?" Hawk asked. Several people nodded their heads.

"Na— I mean Eagle, no, you can't do this. You are too young. It's too dangerous and risky. No," Raven said.

"Come on, Raven, please. I'll finally be able to prove myself to the team and help save the world! Don't you want me to save the world?" Nate pleaded. Raven sighed but finally gave in.

Meanwhile, in *my* head, I wasn't sure what to think. My best friend, 17 year-old Nate, was going to risk his life by getting an eye transplant, purposely get caught by the Destruction, and then be taken to their base. I don't think I've met anyone as brave as that.

Pretty soon people were leaving and some even congratulated Nate. Others just nodded as if they were getting ready for his funeral. When we were leaving I finally had a chance to talk to Nate.

"Are you sure you want to do this?" I asked.

He just nodded.

"I'm going to try everything I can to help you, buddy; I might even come with you!" Even as I said it I doubted myself. But I was still going to try.

Nate still said nothing. He just kept on walking straight ahead as if he was in his own little world. "Are you scared?" I whispered. "I'm sure I would never have been half as brave as you to volunteer,"

"But you did. Right after I did," he said.

"Well I'd rather go then let you risk your life," I said, "But still, it's okay to feel scared,"

Nate sighed, "Call it courage,"

Call it courage. Now *that* was a brave thing to say.

Chapter 10

Later that night, Hawk went over the procedures involved in Nate's eye implantation. They were to perform the operation the next day in another part of Darnis.

I couldn't sleep, and I knew that Nate couldn't either. It was a big day tomorrow, then there would be more things to get ready for the rebellion.

I kept thinking about Nate; and his responsibility. I knew he couldn't do this alone. Tomorrow I was going to convince Hawk to let me go with Nate. I mean, I can't just let my best friend in the whole world just sneak into a top secret government base and risk his life…alone. I smiled mischievously.

****

"Let's go Nate, time for the eye implant," Raven said. He had a sad look in his eyes, and we all knew why. There was a big chance Nate would not come back from his mission.

We got dressed and drove to Darnis. The car ride was awkward and silent. We were all worried the operation might not go as planned.

When we got there, Hawk greeted us. He had a two small security cards in his hands.

"These are for you two, so we don't have that problem again," Hawk said, giving us each one. "Get ready Nate, and be at the operation room in five minutes.

Since we had our cards, Nate and I decided to go to the operation room by ourselves. We went inside the elevator.

Luckily, there was a list of places, offices, and rooms inside the elevator.

I looked down the list so I could look for the operation room. It wasn't there. We looked for surgery or doctors or anything; still, nothing.

"Not again!" Nate groaned. I got mad at Hawk. Why was a he doing this to us? It would have been so much easier if he just told us the level and room!

I looked around the elevator to see if there was any thing that said "Operation Room this floor" but there was none. But I did see something, a small slot. I recognized it as the same one at the Meeting room yesterday! I slide my card inside. It lit up, and we felt the elevator going down.

"You did it!" said Nate.

Suddenly the elevator doors opened. I had never seen this floor before, but we stepped off anyway.

There were no signs or anything. Just hallways and doors. "Here we go again..."

Chapter 11

I approached a random door. They had those security card checks on them. I slid my card in and tried the door. It didn't open. I tried another door, the same. Nate also went to different doors, and still the same results.

Finally, I heard Nate yell, "I got it!" I turned to find him standing in front of a door; the door was open a little.

'If we have to do this one more time, I'm going to kill Hawk! He really needs to stop doing this to us," I say.

"Maybe he's doing on it on purpose to see if we could figure it out ourselves?" Nate said.

I pushed the door open.

It was definitely a room for surgery. Machines were everywhere, hooked up to different things. The walls were white. Doctors rushed about, carrying many kinds of equipment. We stepped in the room. I saw Hawk standing there, waiting for us. I rolled my eyes at him.

He came over to us. "Come on Nate, we need to go into surgery right away, so the DOs won't suspect anything. The faster we perform the operation, the sooner we can finish our mission," Hawk said.

"Good luck," I told Nate, patting his back awkwardly. *What was I supposed to say? 'I hope nothing goes wrong and you don't die in the operation?' I couldn't just say anything like that.*

"Yeah..." Nate said, nodding. He turned and walked into a room where Hawk was waiting for him.

A nurse told me to sit down on some chairs nearby until Nate was finished.

An hour went by, but they were still in surgery. Two hours, maybe more; until finally, Nate appeared at the door. I stood up to greet him.

He smiled at me. I looked up in his eyes to see which one had the implant, but they both looked the same. I raised my eyebrow at him.

"Can't you tell?" Nate said, grinning.

"Nope," I said. I looked at his eyes more closely. The left eye looked pretty normal, but as I studied the right eye, I noticed something like an out line around the pupil. A contact!

"Contacts!" I exclaimed.

"Yup, they changed their mind at the last minute. It took long because we had to test all the things it could do. I need to wait before I can put it on the other eye so I get used to them slowly. They gave me a whole bag just in case," He said, holding up a zip log bag.

Maybe I can still go with Nate. If I wore one of those contacts, I would be just as powerful and then, maybe, I could find my mom.

Chapter 12

The later that day, there was another meeting. We were discussing the plans of attack. Word had already been sent out to the other places where Samsa was located. Apparently there was supposed to be an all-out country rebellion where everybody attacked at the same time.

Before anyone could speak, I decided to take the bull by its horns. "Hawk, I want to go with Nate,"

"What? The job only needs one person, and we can't risk it," he said.

"Well I want to help find my mom, and I know that Nate will need my help, too," I said firmly.

"Yeah, I do need his help. One more is ok, and what if I chicken out? We need someone there to finish the job," Nate piped in.

Hawk sighed, "All right, fine. But you will need to have the implant,"

"Ok, I can do it,"

"Now, we need to discuss the plan of 'Arrest'. We should try simple things at first, then we'll get them to break more rules," Hawk started.

"How about the Circuit? They can attempt a break in, obviously they get caught, then they'll get Arrested," someone said.

There were murmurs among everybody. The Circuit was basically where the DOs lived, or were made. Many people have tried to break in in the past. All were Arrested.

"It's too dangerous. They're only kids, remember?" Hawk said.

"No. We can do it," I said. I was ready to prove myself.

"We'll work something out," Hawk said. "Meeting dismissed,"

***

"Ok, you know what you need to do," Hawk said, right before he dropped us off near the Circuit.

We both nodded.

"Good luck, and remember, don't be scared. Just do it,"

This is might not be so bad.

I turned and started walking. This could be the last thing I ever did on this earth.

Chapter 13

"Ok here's what we should do, I'll be a distraction, and while the DOs chase me, you try to break through the door, and I'll run in behind you. All we need to do is get inside," I said.

"Sounds good to me," Nate said. We both sounded positive, but we knew better. We were scared to death.

"Here goes..." I mumble. I spot a DO standing in front of the door. I pause for a moment, and then break out into a run. I started yelling as if my life depended on it, and it did.

I heard the DO chasing me and telling me to stop, but I kept running. Out of the corner of my eye, I saw Nate standing at the door trying to open it. On the other side of him was a bunch of DOs heading his way.

"Nate!" I yell.

He turns toward me, does something to the door, then gives out a bird whistle. I see him stepping into the Circuit. I ran in after him and we crashed into each other.

I lifted my head up and rubbed my eyes. When everything got into focus, I looked around.

We were surrounded by DOs. They all had guns, or tasers, and other different things I've never seen before.

"Uh...," that's all I said before I felt something shoot into my arm. I could feel myself blacking out, but not before I thought, *Mission accomplished.*

****

I opened my eyes. Everything was so bright. I tried to get up, but then I noticed my hands were handcuffed. I tried turning my head to see where Nate was, but I felt something on my neck. It wasn't choking me; It just had a very tight grip.

I craned my neck as much as I could and saw Nate lying on the ground next to me. That's when I realized where we were. In a really bright room. On my left and right there was two DOs, and when I looked straight ahead, there was another one who was just starring at me. They were all starring at me.

I saw one of those weapons that I had never seen before, and felt pain on my leg.

Oh well, might as well sleep.

Chapter 14

I opened my eyes to find that I wasn't in that room anymore, but I was walking. It was that thing on me. It was making me do things. I looked to the right to see a sleeping Nate, who was also walking, asleep, but walking from the brace around his neck.

After walking forever, we finally came to a halt. They looked like little cells. The DOs threw me in one, and Nate in the other, then walked away.

I went to the farthest corner of the cell and sat down. I tried to remember how many times I was supposed to blink, to get the contact to get me to talk to Nate. I blinked three times.

"Hey Nate, can you hear me?" I whispered quietly.

"Yeah," He said, still groggy from sleep.

"They work! So did you by chance see where they took us?" I asked.

"Nope. They shot me with that thing," He said.

"Should we contact Samsa now?"

"We should wait a little bit longer, see what happens,"

Suddenly the cell doors opened and DOs came in. they pulled me up and dragged me along with them. From all I could hear of Nate's struggling, I knew they were doing the same thing to him.

We walked until we reached this room where hundreds, if not thousands of prisoners sat, and they were...eating? Was this like a cafeteria or something?

All the DOs but one left my side. I could suddenly feel myself being forced to walk. I noticed that all the prisoners had at least one DO with them. I got to the table of food and started putting things on my plate.

The DO took the plate out of my hand. He took something out of his pocket; it looked like a bar code scanner, and scanned it on my brace. That's when I noticed the brace had a number it on it. The DO started refilling my plate with different food, less I noticed, and then walked me up to a table.

Hey maybe I could find my mom or dad here!

I noticed that all the tables were labeled with names on them. Mine, I saw, was the name of my city.

Suddenly I heard, "Danny, is that you?"

Mom?

Chapter 15

I turned to see where the voice was coming from. Then I saw her. There was my mom, standing next to an older man. I ran to her, not caring about the DO, or the Destruction, or anything.

I hugged my mother really hard. Then I looked up at the man. "Dad?"

I hugged him, too. It was as if nothing in the world mattered, only that I was safe with my family. I was so overcome with joy; but then I felt my legs being pulled and I was walking away from them, and I yelled for them, but no matter what I couldn't walk back to them. And not even to my table, but back to my lonely old cell, the DO shutting the door tightly behind me.

***

When Nate came back was when I decided to talk to him again.

"I think we should call *now*," I said.

"Ok. You can call them," he said.

"No, you should call them; it was your mission in the first place," I told him. Nate hung up with me and called Samsa.

Later that night, I heard someone walking toward my cell. My door swung open and a man stood there.

"Dad?" I asked,

"Yes Danny, it's me," he said, coming in.

"How did you get out of your cell?"

"When you've been trapped in this place for this long, you know how to get around," he said. "So, what are you doing here?"

I told him the whole story, starting from when Mom was taken. He only nodded.

But Dad, if you can move around this easily, why don't you just escape?"

"I could, but not without a plan. And with the help of your Mom, we have been planning something that's supposed to happen in four days,"

"Four days? That's the day Samsa is supposed to attack,"

"Attack? What's this about an attack?

"Before Mom was taken she told me the numbers 836, at Samsa they got that as the date we were supposed to attack,"

"Oh, no. this is not supposed to happen," Dad said, shaking his head.

"What's wrong?" I asked.

"I have to go now son, I'll see you tomorrow," he said, rushing out.

"Bye Dad," I mumbled to myself

Chapter 16

It was as if the DOs were trying to keep me from my parents. I didn't see them at all during the meals. But later that night, Dad came to see me again,

"Do you have any sort of communication with Samsa?" he asked.

I told him about our contacts.

"Great, I need you to tell them this," he told me and I told Samsa.

"So Dad, how did you and Mom communicate?" I asked.

"Danny, the Dove can do anything," my dad said smiling.

"The Dove? Wait, you mean, Mom is the Dove?" I asked. *How come no one told me?* Dad nodded.

"So she started Samsa?"

"Nope, I did. Some other guys and I started it, but it wasn't what it is now that's for sure,"

"So what's the plan?"

"Well those of us who have been here longer, knew something like this was going to happen, so we did some things and if we wanted it to, this place could explode right now,"

I felt my jaw drop. "But we would all die though,"

"Well there is no way someone could survive it. After we detonate, then Samsa knows what to do. Then we will be free of the Destruction,"

"How do you know this will work?"

"We don't. That's why we have to do it. This base has more DOs than any of the other bases. So if we take out this place, we take out a large number of them. We would have a chance,"

"Do the people here know that they are going to die?"

"Oh yes, people have known for years,"

"Ok then..," I still wasn't sure if I just wanted to just die.

Chapter 17

The next two days passed really fast. My dad and some of his friends secretly told everyone what they were to do. The base was supposed to explode at 6 and three minutes later was when Samsa was supposed to strike.

Then the day came. Everybody was anxious. Everyone, it seems, except for my

Mom; who was reassuring people and helping with everything.

I wondered how Nate is feeling right now. I've been acting so happy to finally have a family again that I totally forgot about him.

"Hey Nate, so what do you feel about all this?"

'I just want to get this over with,"

"Yeah, me too," I sighed.

"Imagine if we make it back, we would be welcomed as heroes!"

"We sure would, buddy, we sure would," I smiled.

Suddenly the clock struck 6:01. There were two minutes until the explosion.

Everyone was running about, some people were screaming. Even I hadn't realized how close the time was. DOs were running everywhere, shooting people with the things. I spotted my mother and father huddled on the floor along with many others. I grabbed Nate and ran to them.

"Remember boys, whatever happens, we still love you. You too, Nate," my mom said.

6:02.

I huddled with my family and Nate. One of Dad's friends was going to press a button that caused everything to explode. You could hear people crying and screaming.

6:03

Epilogue

Samsa.

The dream that we thought of ten years ago.

The dream of rebellion. Of freedom. Of life.

The dream that is now a reality.

Has come true.

I remember that day, ten years ago, when Jason was Arrested. Before, we had talked about Samsa. But before he was going start….

I then knew that I had to. For Jason. For Danny.

It was dangerous. We all knew that; but when it came to the choice of living in fear and death, we chose freedom and courage instead.

We were going to win.

Ten years later, and we are ending the reality. I looked at my son Danny. How hard it must have been for him; all these years without a father. How confused he must have been, to find out that his parents were the start of something new. A better life. A new world.

I hugged them both tightly, reaching for Nate to join.

I knew this was coming. It had to, and it wasn't fair that Danny and Nate had to pay the price. But this is the way things had to be.

BOOM.

About the Book

Imagine living in a time where a new species takes over your world. They have all the power and you if break one of their rules, you get Arrested. The thing is, when you get Arrested, nobody knows what happens to you because you never come back. This species is the Destruction.

Danny's father was Arrested when Danny was little. Not willing to give up, Danny's mother decided to start a rebel group to overthrow the Destruction, and end them once and for all.

What happens? Does the rebellion work? Do they reunite with Danny's father? Read on to find out what happens next!

About the Author

Eman Ghoneim is a 13 year old writer. She goes to Lexington Universal Academy, a small private Islamic school in Lexington, Kentucky. She loves to read and write and loves being creative and original in her work. This is her third novel. She hopes that one day she will have a future in writing.

Made in the USA
Las Vegas, NV
30 January 2025